Printed in China

First Edition
1 3 5 7 9 10 8 6 4 2

T425-2382-5-12290
ISBN 978-1-4231-7946-7

For more Disney Press fun, visit www.disneybooks.com
This book was printed on paper created from a sustainable source.

DISNEY · PIXAR

Ride 'em,
Cowboy!

by Kate McMullan

Illustrated by Lorelay Bove

Disney PRESS

New York

Cowboy Bob rode the bull for eight seconds, Andy read to his toys. *Cowboy Bob won the Silver Buckle. He was the rodeo champ!*

"Andy!" called his mom. "Into the car or we'll be late for the rodeo."

"Yee-haw!"

yelled Andy, and he raced from the room.

"Rodeo time!"

yelled Woody.

"Yahoo!" cried Jessie. "I'm the fastest rope in the West!"

"Care to pit your skills against mine, cowgirl?" Woody asked.

"You're on!" said Jesse.

"**Aw right!**" cried Slinky Dog. "We're havin' a rodeo!"

"Let's get organized," called Buzz. "Rodeo ring right here. Chute over there. Everybody ready? First event—Steer Wrestling!"

"Uh . . . how 'bout a
practice run?" said Woody.
"Don't worry, Woody,"
coached Slinky Dog. "Just
take him down fast."

"Go!" called Buzz.
"Yee-haw!" cried Woody
as he and Bullseye burst out
of the chute.
"Moooo!" said Hamm.
"I say, moo!" He jumped
on a skate.

Hamm sped away from Woody. He hit a log, and it went flying.
"Look out, Woody!" yelled Slinky.
"Bullseye—jump!" cried Woody.
Bullseye leaped over the log and galloped closer to "the steer."

Woody sprang off his horse and onto Hamm. He tried to wrestle him to the ground.

"Uhhhh," Woody groaned.

"Give it up, Woody," said Hamm. "I'm packin' twelve-fifty in quarters."

Next it was Jessie's turn. She whistled for Bullseye and jumped on his back. "Yee-haw!" she cried, galloping after the steer.

"**What, again?**" cried Hamm, and he took off running. Bullseye caught up with Hamm.

Jessie jumped onto Hamm's back. She held on to his change slot with one hand and tickled his belly with the other. **"Kitchykitchy-koo!"** she cried.

"Hoo-hoo-hah!" Hamm laughed. He rolled onto his side. **"Hoo-hoo! That tickles!"**

"Nice wrestlin', little lady," said Buzz. "Next up, Barrel Racing. **Barrels?**"

The Little Green Aliens lined up.

"Jessie? You're first," called Buzz. "Go!"

Jessie rode into the ring. She guided Bullseye around the barrels and back again without knocking any of them over.

"Fourteen seconds!" cried Buzz.

"Beat that, cowboy," said Jessie.
"Watch me, cowgirl," said
Woody as he mounted his horse.
"Not too fast, Woody," warned
Slinky.

"Go!" called Buzz.

"Ride like the wind,
Bullseye!" cried Woody.
Bullseye galloped for
the barrels.
"Oooooooooh!"
cried the aliens.

"Faster, Bullseye!" shouted Woody. "We have to win!" Bullseye galloped faster.

"Ooooooooh!" The aliens hunkered down and shut their eyes.

But Bullseye whizzed past the aliens and galloped out the door.

"Aw, great!" said Slinky Dog. **"Just great!"**

"The winner is **Jessie!**" announced Buzz.

"Yay!" cheered the toys.

"Thanks a lot, Bullseye," muttered Woody.

"Last event—Bull Riding!" said Buzz. "Sarge? Call the bull!"

"Sir! Yes, sir!" said Sarge. He whistled.

Buster nosed open the door and ran into Andy's room.

"Bull reporting for duty, sir!" Sarge added.

"Think you can ride that bull for eight seconds, cowboy?" asked Jessie.

"Nothin' to it, cowgirl," said Woody.

Woody climbed onto Buster's back.

"Ready, set, go!" Buzz called.

Buster jumped out of the chute and ran around the ring.

"Ride 'em, cowboy!" yelled Slinky.

"Hey, Jessie!" cried Woody. "Anything you can do, I can do, too!" And he stood up on Buster's back.

"Sit down, Woody!" cried Slinky.

Woody began to wobble.

"Ahhhhhhh!"
Woody cried as he flew off
Buster's back.
**"To infinity and
beyond!"** called Buzz.

SPLAT!

Woody hit the wall and slid down.

Slinky Dog ran over.

"You okay, Woody?"

"Yeahhhhh," said Woody.

"Next rider!" called Buzz.
"Yeeeeee-haaaaa!" yelled Jessie.

She held tight as
Buster bucked and
kicked and raced
around Andy's room.

"Eight seconds
are up!" said Buzz.
"We have our rodeo
champ!"

"For a prize?" said Buzz. "I'd—uh—like you to have my Star Command belt buckle."

"Thanks a heap, spaceman!" exclaimed Jessie.

Buzz grinned. "Any time, cowgirl!"

Afterward, Woody caught up with Jessie.

"Well, you beat me fair and square, cowgirl," he said.

"This time, cowboy," said Jessie. "But there's always next time."

Seconds later, Andy galloped into his room.

He grabbed Woody and Jessie. **"Rodeo time!"** he cried. "Which one of you is gonna be the rodeo champ?"

You know, it doesn't matter who's champ, thought Woody. It's all about having fun with the other cowpokes. **Yee-haw!**